The Little Snowflake

by Mark Skewes Van Doren

Very early one cold, crisp,
Christmas morning,
Way up high
In the middle of a huge cloud,
A little snowflake was born.

And before the sun even rose that morning,
the Little Snowflake found itself falling.
Swirling back and forth in the wind,
But falling,
Steadily falling.

It wasn't alone, that Little Snowflake, no.
It was surrounded by millions and millions
of other snowflakes.

Falling was the only thing the brand new
Little Snowflake had ever known. So when
suddenly it stopped, it was a major shock!
"Whoa!" said the Little Snowflake.
"What was that? What just happened?"
"We hit the ground, silly!" said a big,
friendly snowflake nearby.

The Little Snowflake could see who had spoken, because just then the sun had begun to rise over the frozen winter morning.

They were BEAUTIFUL,
thought the Little Snowflake.
Made of crystals with
all sorts of fancy patterns.
"There are SO many snowflakes!"

"And did you know?" said the big snowflake,
"that no two of us are exactly alike?
Some of us look alike,
but no two snowflakes are the same.
We are all unique."

"You mean we're all SPECIAL?"
asked the Little Snowflake.
"That's right!" said the big snowflake.
"You're not just like ANY other snowflake
in the whole wide world.
You are special!"
The Little Snowflake beamed with pride.

From somewhere beyond, the Little Snowflake
heard children's voices. Then the whole world
started rolling, tumbling, end over end.
"What's going on?" the frightened
Little Snowflake cried.
"It's okay! Don't worry," said the big snowflake.
"It's just kids, they're making a snowman!"

"Oh!" said the Little Snowflake,
having no idea what that meant
until the big snowflake explained.
"Life is short.
Love every moment!
And have fun!"
the big snowflake added cheerfully.

And that was how,
on that cold, crisp, Christmas morning,
the Little Snowflake found itself part
of the top ball of a snowman.
Right next to the carrot
that served as the snowman's nose.

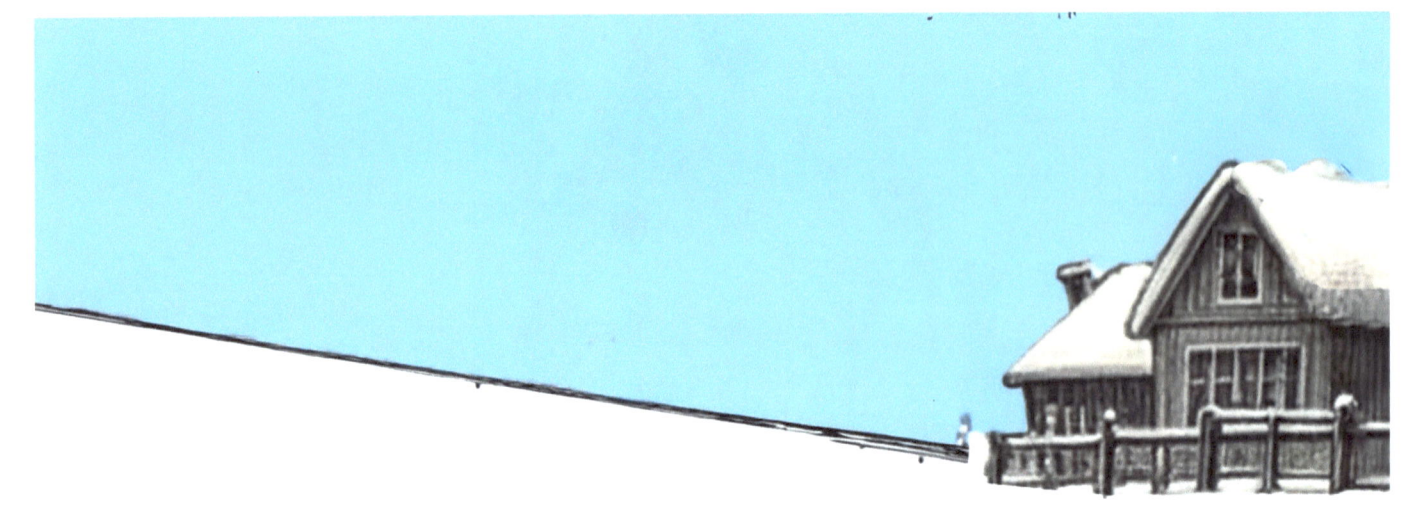

The Little Snowflake was pleased to be a part of the
children's snowman that made them so happy.
And the kids came out to play in the snow every day.
At night they would scamper back to their
houses beside the field.
But the next morning they would be back,
laughing and screaming with delight.

Until one day there was silence.
"What's going on? What happened? Where are
all the children?" asked the Little Snowflake.
"Christmas vacation is over," said the big
snowflake. "They're back in school."
"Oh," said the Little Snowflake, a bit sadly.

And then, something terrible happened.
The days, got warmer.
And the snowman, began to melt.

The Little Snowflake watched, wide-eyed,
as one by one, all the snowflakes around them
began to melt into drops of water and merge into
rivulets, streaming to the ground.
"What's happening?" cried the Little
Snowflake. "I'm scared!"

"Don't worry!" the big snowflake said,
comfortingly. "It's natural.
We're just going back
to where we came from."

"But I'm a SNOWFLAKE!
I'm SPECIAL!
There's no one just like me!"
the Little Snowflake protested.
Then, just before melting,
the big snowflake said:

"Listen to me, Little Snowflake!
All is well,
have FAITH!
We're just going back to the cloud.
But don't worry, we'll be back.
Someday soon!"

And so,
With Faith in it's heart
the Little Snowflake,
Melted.

But the very next year,
Way up high
In the middle of a huge cloud
On a cold, crisp, Christmas morning...

NOT
THE
END

www.ingramcontent.com/pod-product-compliance
Lightning Source LLC
Chambersburg PA
CBHW041135100726
47911CB00003B/136